D0590111

Postman Pat
Gets a Pet

Story by **John Cunliffe**   Pictures by **Joan Hickson**
From the original Television designs by **Ivor Wood**

Scholastic Children's Books,
Scholastic Publications Ltd,
7-9 Pratt Street, London NW1 0AE, UK

Scholastic Inc.,
730 Broadway, New York, NY 10003, USA

Scholastic Canada Ltd,
123 Newkirk Road, Richmond Hill,
Ontario, Canada L4C 3G5

Ashton Scholastic Pty Ltd,
PO Box 579, Gosford, New South Wales,
Australia

Ashton Scholastic Ltd,
Private Bag 1, Penrose, Auckland,
New Zealand

First published in the UK by Scholastic Publications Ltd, 1989
This edition published 1993
Text copyright © John Cunliffe 1989 and 1993
Illustrations copyright © Scholastic Publications Ltd and Woodland
Animations Limited, 1989

A longer version of this story has been previously published as
a Handy Hippo

ISBN: 0 590 54145 5

10 9 8 7 6 5 4 3 2 1

Printed in Hong Kong by Paramount Printing Group Ltd.

There was a time, long ago, when Pat had no cat. He was alone in his red van, and he had no Jess to talk to as he drove along. But the story really begins with three white mice...

One day, they all went shopping, when Julian saw something that made his eyes shine.

"Look!"

It was a cage full of mice. One of the mice was looking out at Julian, and twitching its whiskers.

4

"Ooooh," said Pat, "I'm not sure I like mice."

"I always wanted one when I was little," said Sara, "but my mum would never let me."

"I'd *love* a mouse," said Julian.

"You'd need two or three, to keep each other company," said Sara. "Well, we could go in and look at them."

So they did.

"Aren't they lovely?" said Julian.

"Mmmmmm...." said Pat. "I'm not too sure...Ouch!"

A little grey mouse had given his finger a good nip.

"You frightened it," said Sara. "That's why it bit you. They have to get used to you."

"I don't think I could," said Pat.

"Can we....?" said Julian.

"Well...they are lovely," said Sara. "Yes, all right then."

And she bought all four mice, and a cage to keep them in.

"What shall we call them?" said Julian.

"You can call that one Nipper," said Pat.

"And the white ones are Bess and Bill," said Julian.

"And the black-and-white one's Jess," said Sara.

It was soon time to catch the bus home to Greendale. It was almost full. The Reverend Timms jumped in, just as the bus was getting ready to start.

"Hello," he said, "what have you got there? Mice? Bless me, I had some when I was a boy. What a lovely present."

Julian put the cage of mice on the seat
beside him. He looked out of the window
to wave at Peter Fogg on his tractor. When
he looked back at the mice, there was
Nipper, sitting on top of the cage, looking
all about him with great interest.

He had never seen a bus before, and meant to find out all about it. Nipper jumped off the cage, ran along the seat, up the back, and jumped into Dorothy Thompson's lap. She screamed, "A mouse! A mouse! Help!"

She jumped up, shaking Nipper off her coat and onto the floor. Now it ran between the Reverend's legs. It was away along the length of the bus, making people jump and squeal as it tickled their feet. The driver stopped the bus and joined in the hunt for the mouse.

Everyone tried to catch that little mouse. And whilst they were busy, the other three squeezed out between the bars of the cage, and ran for freedom. What a rumption there was!

It was the Reverend Timms who put things to rights, in the end. He said, in his best church voice, "Dear friends. If you will all sit still and quiet I'll catch those mice in a trice. I kept mice as a boy, and I know what to do." At the sound of his voice, everyone calmed down and sat quietly.

The Reverend borrowed a plastic bucket from Granny Dryden, and some crumbs of cake from Miss Hubbard. He put the cake in the bucket and the bucket on the floor, sideways, and waited. Everyone sat very still. You would have thought there was no-one in that bus, it was so quiet. But you could hear a scurrying and a scratching, as the four mice explored the bus. And then a patter-patter sound, when they found the bucket, and their little paws tapped on the smooth plastic. Then a tiny munching sound, as they ate the cake.

The Reverend picked up the bucket quickly. There were the four little mice, in the bottom, and no matter what they did, they could not get out again. The plastic was too slippery for them to climb.

The mice had to live in the bucket for a day or two, until Pat could think what to do.

When Mrs Goggins heard about the trouble with the mice, she said, "If you get a bigger pet it won't squeeze between the bars. Why don't you get a hamster? They're lovely."

So Pat went to Pencaster on Tuesday afternoon, and changed the mice for a lovely golden hamster.

One day, Julian said, "Do you think we could let it out for a run round the carpet?"

Sara said, "Well, I'm sure it wouldn't do any harm to let it out for a little while, if you keep your eye on it. It's too big to go down a mouse-hole."

But the hamster went behind the settee, and wouldn't come out. When they looked behind the settee the hamster had gone.

Then Pat came home and said, "What's this hole?"

Sara said, "What hole?....Oh!"

When Ted called in, they showed him the hole.

"That's a hamster-hole, all right," he said. "Perhaps our Towser could get it out."

He brought his little dog in. It snuffled at the hole, and wagged its tail like mad, but it couldn't get the hamster out.

But Pat had an idea.

"I'll catch that hamster," he said.

"You'll never get it in a bucket," said Ted.

"No, but I bet you I can get it," said
Pat.

That night, Pat got the old baby-bath
out, and put it near to the hole the hamster
had made. He put some hamster-food in the
empty bath. Then he found a long piece of
wood and leaned it against the side. The
wood made a path up to the edge of the
bath.

"Are you thinking of giving that
hamster a bath?" said Sara.

"It might need one," said Pat. "But it must be getting hungry. When we've gone to bed, it's sure to come out. The idea is, that it will walk up the wood, jump in the bath for the food, and not be able to climb out again up the slippery sides."

"It'll never work," said Sara, "hamsters have more brains than mice."

When all the house was quiet, there was a tiny sound of little paws and nibbling teeth. Pat crept downstairs, with his torch. There, in the empty bath, sat a dusty hamster, blinking in the light!

On Wednesday afternoon, Pat took the hamster back to Pencaster in its cage, and came back with a large sheep-dog.

Julian called the dog Bess, after one of the mice. He loved her. She was a very lively dog, and had to go for a long walk, every day. When Pat was out with his letters, and Julian was at school, Sara and Bess walked the hills all over Greendale. Then Sara got a job in Pencaster. What about Bess?

"She'll have to come with me, in my van," said Pat.

But, oh dear, Bess was hopeless in Pat's van. She wouldn't stay in her basket. She chewed the corner of a parcel, one day. She jumped out and chased hens. She ran off looking for sheep to round up, and it took Pat an hour to find her.

"Major Forbes is on the look-out for another sheep-dog," said Miss Hubbard. "And he's a dab at training dogs. He'd soon get her into shape. Why don't you have a word with him?"

"I will," said Pat.

Major Forbes was delighted.

"She's just the dog for me," he said.
"Bring her round on Monday, and we'll
make a start with her."

So it was all settled. But Pat, and Sara, and Julian were sad. They would miss Bess, far more than they had missed the hamster or the mice.

Monday came. Julian looked tearful as he said, "Goodbye," to Bess.

"Don't take on," said Pat. "You'll be able to go round to the Major's to see her, any time you like."

"I know," said Julian, but he still looked sad.

It was time to take Bess to Major
Forbes. Pat drove along, with Bess by his
side. Just as they were passing Alf
Thompson's bottom meadow, Bess began to
make a fuss.

"Oh, you don't want to get out, do
you?" said Pat. "Just when we're late."

But Bess did want to get out. She barked and whined until Pat stopped the van.

"Be quick, then," said Pat.

Bess jumped out. But she still whined at Pat.

"What is it now?" said Pat in a cross voice.

She wanted him to get out and look. Pat came. Bess led him to a cardboard box, stuck in the hedge. She sniffed and whined and wagged her tail. She nosed at the box.

"What is it, Bess?" said Pat.
Pat lifted the lid of the box.

"Well, I'll be blessed!" said Pat. "How did you know that was there?"

Curled up in the bottom of the box was a little black and white kitten. Pat picked it up gently, and it opened its eyes and mewed at him.

"Poor little thing," said Pat. "Who can have left you there?"

Bess gave it a kiss with her long wet tongue that made it sneeze.

"Good girl," said Pat.

And this is how Pat arrived home that day, without Bess, but with a kitten tucked up in his warm coat.

"Let's call it Jess," said Julian.

And they did. They all loved Jess. He didn't run away, or chase hens, or chew holes in the floor, or make people scream in the bus. He has ridden in the van every day with Pat, from that day to this. Pat says, "He's grand company, is our Jess."

As for Bess, she became a very good sheep-dog. She loves nothing better than a good day out working the sheep on the fells; and the shepherd often brings her to see Pat, and Sara, and Julian... and her old friend Jess.